WHEN THE MOON IS FULL

A LUNAR YEAR

WHEN THE MOON IS FULL

BY PENNY POLLOCK   ILLUSTRATED BY MARY AZARIAN

Little, Brown and Company • Boston New York London

Full moons come,
full moons go,
softening nights
with their silver glow.
They pass in silence,
all untamed,
but as they travel,
they are named.

JANUARY
THE WOLF MOON

The weather chills,
the night is long,
wolf lifts his head
in lonely song.
His notes float high,
his notes drift low,
mournful in the
moonlight glow.

*Native Americans believed that
wolves became restless in January.*

FEBRUARY
THE SNOW MOON

Snow falls all day
into the night
snuggling the world
in downy white.
Old Man Moon
hides his face
behind a curtain
of winter's lace.

*February is a month of
heavy snow.*

MARCH
THE SAP MOON

Cold nights,
warm days,
sap is sure to run.
Moon looms in
the branches,
waiting for the sun.

*Native Americans and the
early European settlers collected
sap for syrup in March.*

APRIL
THE FROG MOON

Frogs sit in the marshes,
throats bellowed tight,
feeling quite romantic,
calling through the night.
Come my love, my love, my love.
Come be mine tonight.

*In April life bursts forth
following the cold of winter.*

MAY
THE FLOWER MOON

Lilies of the valley
ring each silent bell
when May's bright moon
lightens up the dell.
Furry-footed creatures
scurry here and there
dancing to the music
they can hear
quite well.

Many flowers bloom in May.

JUNE
THE STRAWBERRY MOON

We feast all night
in moon's spotlight
forgetting all our foes,
tramping on the berries
that squish between our toes.

Strawberries ripen in June.
Native Americans and the European
settlers collected wild berries.

PICK YOUR OWN

JULY
THE BUCK MOON

Young bucks
in the hayfield,
antlers held aloft.
Moonbeams slanting down,
show them velvet soft.

Bucks sprout their first
antlers in July.

AUGUST
THE GREEN CORN MOON

Moonbeams touch the cornfield,
laying shadows stripe by stripe
down the endless rows of corn,
tall and green and ripe.

*Corn was the basic food for most
Native Americans. It ripens in August.
Many tribes celebrated the
Green Corn Festival.*

SEPTEMBER
THE HARVEST MOON

Squirrel rests in an ancient oak,
tail wrapped round her like a cloak,
looking over the moonlit field
where Mother Earth's generous yield
of endless acorns, nuts, and seeds
is quite enough to meet all needs.

*September marks the final gathering
of most crops. This is celebrated
in many cultures.*

OCTOBER
THE HUNTER'S MOON

Hush, young hare,
beware, take care.
Danger fills the night.
Pray a cloud will shade
the moon,
putting out its light.

In October the moon rises quickly,
adding to the light of the setting sun. This
gives hunters extra time to hunt.

NOVEMBER
THE BEAVER MOON

Black and icy pond
mirrors moon so round,
while hidden in the beavers' lodge
coziness abounds.

Beavers were important to
Native Americans, who hunted them
for food and to sell their skins.

DECEMBER
THE LONG NIGHT MOON

December moon floats on
cloud's crest
as if to take
a little rest.
No one sees this,
no one knows
except some sleepy-eyed
old crows.

December nights are the longest
nights of the year.

BLUE MOONS AND MORE
QUESTIONS AND ANSWERS ABOUT THE MOON

Why do full moons have names?
The Native Americans kept time by the Moon. They knew that every month had a full moon, so "many moons" meant many months. They chose names that reflected something special about each of these time periods. The elders passed along the names, mainly through storytelling.

Who made up the names of moons?
Many of the names come from the Native Americans. Different tribes use different names. Some names come from European-American folklore.

Can a full moon have more than one name?
Yes, often a full moon has several names. Here are some examples:

January:	Old Moon
February:	Hunger Moon
March:	Crow Moon
April:	Grass Moon
May:	Planting Moon
June:	Rose Moon
July:	Hay Moon
August:	Grain Moon
September:	Fruit Moon
October:	Harvest Moon
November:	Frosty Moon
December:	Moon before Yule

Is there a man in the Moon?
No, but sometimes when the Moon is full it looks a little like a man's face. This is caused by the craters (big holes), mountains, and plains on the Moon.

What is the Moon made of?
It is made of rock.

Has anyone gone to the Moon?
Yes. Astronauts Neil Armstrong and Edwin Aldrin were the first to walk on the Moon, on July 20, 1969.

Can people live on the Moon?
Maybe someday people will live on the Moon. It will be difficult because there is no water or air. The nights are freezing. The days are boiling hot.

Why is the Moon silver-white?
It reflects light from the Sun.

Is it safe to look at the Moon?
Yes, but please do not look directly at the Sun. It will hurt your eyes.

Does the Moon stay still?
No, the Moon circles Earth once each month. Also, the Moon and Earth move together around the Sun. It takes one year for Earth and the Moon to travel around the Sun.

Why does the Moon change shape?
It does not change shape. It appears to change shape because, as the Moon moves around Earth, the Sun shines on different parts of the Moon. This changing amount of light causes the phases of the Moon. When the Sun shines on all of the Moon we see a full moon.

What is a lunar eclipse?
A lunar eclipse occurs when Earth blocks the Sun's light, leaving the Moon in shadow.

Do we see both sides of the Moon?
No, we see only one side. This is the side that always faces Earth. Astronomers call it the near side. They call the other side the far side.

Is the Moon visible all night, every night?
No, sometimes it is visible only in the evening, or only very late at night, or even during the daytime.

Which is biggest: the Sun, Earth, or the Moon?
The Sun is the biggest. Earth is much smaller than the Sun, and the Moon is smaller than Earth.

Which is nearer to Earth, the Sun or the Moon?
The Moon is much closer.

Are there twelve full moons every year?
No, sometimes there are thirteen.

What is a blue moon?
By common usage, a blue moon is the second full moon in one month or the fourth in a season. This is not a scientific name, but it is used in phrases such as "once in a blue moon." This means something that happens rarely.

Is a blue moon colored blue?
No, it is silver-white like other moons.

How often does a blue moon appear?
Blue moons occur about every two years and nine months.

FOR GREGORY FORD POLLOCK
WITH LOVE, BABA
— P. P.

TO ELEANOR HATCH AND LAWRENCE SCHNEIDER
WITH GRATITUDE FOR THEIR LOVE AND SUPPORT
— M. A.

Many thanks to Steve Slivan, our MIT moon man,
for his generous advice.

Text copyright © 2001 by Penny Pollock
Illustrations copyright © 2001 by Mary Azarian

First Edition

Library of Congress Cataloging-in-Publication Data
Pollock, Penny.
  When the moon is full / by Penny Pollock ; illustrated by Mary Azarian. — 1st ed.
    p. cm.
  ISBN 0-316-71317-1
  1. Moon — Folklore. 2. Seasons — Folklore. [1. Moon — Folklore. 2. Months —
Folklore.] I. Azarian, Mary, ill. II. Title.
  GR625.P65 2001
  811'.54 — dc21   00-028238

10 9 8 7 6 5 4 3

TWP

Printed in Singapore

The illustrations for this book are hand-colored woodcut prints.
The text was set in Schneidler, and the display typefaces are Penumbra and Sanvito.